Hanged Passions
A Tarot Inspired Tale of MM Romance, Bondage, and Empowerment

Tarot Fantasies
Book Three

Jax Wilder

Hanged Passions

Tarot Fantasies Series
Jax Wilder

RAINBOW QUARTZ PUBLISHING

Published by Rainbow Quartz Publishing

Edmonds WA, 98026

ISBN: 978-1-961714-44-1

First Edition: 2024

Cover design by Miranda Townsend

Interior design by Miranda Townsend

Tarot Card description by Lorelai Hamilton from the book Teenage Tarot – used with permission.

Library of Congress Cataloging-in-Publication Data has been applied for.

This book is a work of nonfiction. Names, characters, places, and incidents are either the product of the author's imagination or used fictitiously. Any resemblance to actual events, locales, or persons, living or dead, is entirely coincidental.

For permissions or inquiries, please contact:

rainbowquartzpublishing@gmail.com

 Created with Vellum

For every person who ever felt less than.
I see you, you sexy thing.
You are worthy of love.

Jax Wilder

12. The Hanged Man

"Shift your mindset and view the situation from a new angle," The Hanged Man.

Key Words and Phrases
Suspension and surrender
Seeing things from a new perspective
Letting go of control
Pause for reflection and introspection
Acceptance of delays or setbacks
Spiritual enlightenment and awakening
Release of old patterns or beliefs
Embracing the present moment

The Hanged Man is about gaining a new perspective. Sometimes you have to look at things from a different angle to really understand them. It's about shifting your mindset and seeing things in a whole new light.

It's not as easy as flipping yourself upside down and calling it a day. It's about surrendering to the moment, letting go of control, and trusting that everything will work out in the end.

—Lorelai Hamilton, author of *Teenage Tarot* and *Tarot Tales & Magic Spells*

ONE

"Do you want to get out of here?" a husky voice with a cheeky smile asked.

I firmly grasped his muscular and well-defined arm, feeling the strength and power within it. "Yes," I said without thinking.

I had only been in this bar for about forty-five minutes, and I was already agreeing to go home with a guy? Not just any guy. This man was an absolute Adonis. Blond curly hair that was neat and trimmed above his beautiful deep blue eyes. Short, perfect button nose I wanted to bite.

"Do you want me to get us an Uber?" I asked as we walked onto the dirty street. The sound of car horns and the smell of exhaust wafted in the air.

"No need," Adonis said, grabbing my hand and leading me around the corner of the building. His hand was soft in mine. My cock swelled at his touch.

My gaze traveled up his arm, past his shoulders,

and finally settled on his exposed, possibly shaved chest. If only my chest was as smooth as a polished stone. His nipples were perky and erect upon his bulky chest. I traced the curve of the valley between his well-defined pecs, my fingertips grazing his warm skin, until my hand reached the chiseled contours of his stomach. From there, my gaze followed the tantalizing "v" shape that swayed with his every step.

We turned down a dark alley. "Where are we heading?" I asked, meeting his eyes.

With a smile that revealed his pearly white teeth and luscious lips, Adonis motioned for me to follow him. "Just over here, handsome."

My mind drifted back to senior prom. I could still see the crowded hallways as couples filtered in. My heart pounded in my chest. The cutest guy in school wanted to be my date. I'd said yes, and when I arrived at prom, his sharp and cruel laugh still echoed in my ears. "You and me? You thought I was serious?" he sneered, eyes glancing around to make sure others were watching. "Not in a million years, Andrew." The humiliation burned just as fresh now as it did then, a constant reminder that people couldn't be trusted.

I willed the excitement coursing through me to stay the course and pushed thoughts of bullies aside. They had no control over me.

We tucked ourselves behind a large, green dumpster. With a sudden, swift motion, Adonis yanked me towards him, pinning me against the wall. His tongue entered my mouth, and I felt myself being pulled under, deeper and deeper. I kissed him back, running my hands up and down his perfectly sculpted chest. His hands traced the outside of my jeans, and his moans grew louder as he caressed my throbbing arousal.

I pulled back a little. "Where are we going to go?"

Adonis flashed another sly smile. "We're already here."

My gaze drifted down as he unbuttoned his white pants. He paused, surveying the alleyway from left to right. Our eyes locked, and in a bold move, Adonis firmly grasped my hand, leading it towards his cock.

The sensation of his throbbing erection pressed against the fabric of his silky boxers was palpable. The tips of my fingers followed the outline of his shaft down towards his balls and massaged them gently. With an arched back, he leaned against the brick wall and rested his shoulder blades on it. I followed the outline of his cock back up towards the tip. Adonis closed his eyes, bit his bottom lip, and emitted a soft moan of pleasure.

"Oh yeah," his voice took on a deep, raspy quality.

My eyes traveled downward to his midsection, and he wasted no time in removing his blue, silky boxers, revealing his erect rod. He reached out and clasped his girth with his right hand, giving it a vigorous up and down.

I paused.

"Come on, you know you want it," he said as he arched back further. He shook his dick at me again.

Nervously, I glanced down the dimly lit alley, my eyes searching for any signs of movement on the street. Was this some kind of fucked-up joke? Anxiety gnawed at me relentlessly, pulling me from the inside. I looked down the opposite alley and saw a few people in the distance, obviously walking by, completely unaware of my existence. I couldn't shake the feeling that I was being punked. What did Adonis see in me?

I lowered myself to the ground, meeting his cock at eye level. He was still firmly clutched onto himself, waving his cock at my face.

"You want to suck that dick?" he asked as he bit his lip again.

I took his cock in my hands, feeling his smooth shaft. My hand replaced his. I glided my hand up and down. I glanced again down the alley, fear burning inside of me.

I brought my attention back to his perfectly chiseled body, my hand still gripping him. I leaned in and opened my mouth.

Licked my lips.

But then I let go and stood up. "I'm sorry. I can't do this. Not here," I said, walking away in the direction we came from. Although I could distinctly hear a sigh of frustration, there was no sound of him trailing behind me.

· · ·

"The alleyway Adonis was two years ago?" Larissa blurted out in the middle of The Arcane Room.

"Shhhhh, Jesus Larissa, can you be any louder?" I have been friends with Larissa since my freshman year of college. She was the first person I came out to, and she still embarrassed me on a near-daily basis.

"This is why we're here," Larissa blurts out, not even a decibel softer.

"To embarrass me?" I asked and felt my cheeks get hot.

"No, to release your inhibitions and free yourself!" Larissa spread her arms wide, nearly knocking over a bottle of green liquid off the shelf. "It's time to move on from the Seans and Adonises of the world."

Leave it to Larissa to bring up the most embarrassing moments of my life. Sean was my boyfriend in college. He wasn't out to his friends or family yet. I was standing in the middle of the room, a red solo cup in hand, when Sean approached me. We weren't public. He wouldn't hardly look at me when attending the same party. But that night had been different.

Sean was charming, flirty, and I was naive enough to believe his words. "I want you. I don't want to hide who I am anymore," he had said. My heart soared, but as soon as we stepped outside, his friends burst out laughing from behind the bushes. "Did you really think he was into you?" they jeered. The shame of that moment still lingered, feeding my mistrust.

I centered myself and pushed the thoughts away.

"I deserve better than assholes. I'm going to free my inhibitions or something." I forced a laugh.

"Damn right you are!" cheered Larissa.

Out of thin air, a mysterious woman suddenly emerged and swiftly snatched the jar out of thin air, preventing it from shattering.

"Freeing inhibitions? Sounds like you found the right place," the woman said with a warm smile.

I shot Larissa a look, my face flushed with embarrassment. "Sorry about that," I mumbled, trying to compose myself. "She can be a bit... enthusiastic."

The shop owner chuckled. Her eyes sparkled with amusement. "No need to apologize. Enthusiasm is welcome here."

Larissa grinned, clearly unfazed by my embarrassment. "See? I told you this place would be perfect for you."

The woman's gaze turned more curious. "So, what brings you to The Arcane Room today?"

I hesitated, glancing at Larissa for support. She nudged me forward, her eyes urging me to speak.

"I... I'm looking for guidance," I finally said, my voice barely above a whisper. "I've been feeling a little lost and stuck in my ways. Something has to change."

The woman nodded understandingly. She had long black hair and wore a flowing dress that accentuated her tattoos. "Follow me, dear." She led us to a counter near the back of the room. "Do you know much about tarot?"

"No," I admitted.

"Here at The Arcane Room, we offer a special…" she paused and met my eyes before continuing, "individualized experience."

She pulled out a deck of cards, much larger than a typical playing deck. She shuffled and laid them out on the table in front of me, backside up. "Choose only one," she said and waved her hand over the deck.

I glanced at Larissa, who nodded encouragingly. My hands trembled as I reached for a card, my mind racing with doubts. What if this was a mistake? What if I made a fool of myself again?

"The Hanged Man," Ms. Vesper breathed. "It represents suspension, letting go, and seeing things from a new perspective."

Her words struck a chord, but fear washed over me. Letting go? I had spent my life trying to control how others saw me, building walls to protect myself. Could I really trust this process? My mind flashed back to the party in college, the punishing laughter of my ex's friends. I couldn't bear to be humiliated again.

It's also probably why I'm still single.

"The Hanged Man," she breathed. "It represents suspension, letting go, and seeing things from a new perspective. Sometimes, the only way to move forward is to stop struggling and simply surrender."

Her words resonated within me. A flicker of hope. "How do I do that?"

The woman stepped closer, her presence electrifying. "I can show you."

"Okay."

Before leading me into a small white room void of decor, she turned to Larissa. "I'll be right back out in a moment. Have a look around the store and I can answer any questions when I return."

Larissa spun on her heels and waved a hand in the air. "I'll just be out here, hitting on the next somethin'-somethin' that walks in."

She motioned for me to have a seat on the black leather chaise lounge in the center of the room. From nowhere, she handed me a clipboard. "I just need you to sign this waiver and then we can begin."

I glanced at the waiver.

By participating, you accept that this simulation may involve physical and emotional sensations... I cocked my head but kept reading. *The experience includes drinking a special tea and a ritual spell casting by Ms. Vesper...* I looked up and she smiled back serenely. *Time within the simulation may feel longer than in reality, though the experience will only last twenty minutes in real-time. By participating, you release The Arcane Room and its staff from any liability for loss, damage, or injury that may occur.*

I gulped, wanting instinctually to leave out of fear. But Larissa trusted this woman. And I came looking to shake things up. So, I signed the waiver.

"I'm Andrew," I said, trying to steady my breathing and the pounding heart in my chest.

"Nice to meet you, Andrew," she took the form

from me and passed me a cup of tea. Ms. Vesper smiled, her gaze intense and knowing. "You selected The Hanged Man. That tells me you're feeling trapped, unable to move forward. But it's more than that. You're inhibited by your fears and insecurities."

I nodded. "Something like that."

"This experience will help you release all of that anxiety you're carrying around so you can get to a place of," she sucked in a breath, "release."

"What exactly is going to happen?" I asked, trepidation evident in my voice.

"You'll drink that tea and then sit back and relax. Everything that happens beyond the tea is up to you. Remember, it's your fantasy, and you are the driver. The magic in this space will take you to a safe and wonderful place where you can live out your deepest and darkest inner desires."

"How much does all this cost?" I asked.

"It's not money that troubles me, but rather the negative energy swirling all around you. If you feel like your experience added something positive to your life, you are welcome to leave gratuity before you leave. Now drink up."

I looked down at the cup of tea in my hands, apprehension bubbling up in every inch of me. Ms. Vesper reached out and covered my hands, her touch sending a welcome shiver down my spine. "There is a path for you, and you will find it."

Her words filled me with hope. I can do this. I can let go. In several rapid gulps, I downed the tea.

"In the stillness of the night, The Hanged Man's

strength, make clear his sight. Suspend fears, let wisdom flow. Through surrender, courage grows. Release doubts, let truth be known. Guide the path where light has shown." Ms. Vesper's voice was raw and laced with magic.

I slumped back into the chaise lounge as the room slipped away.

Two

Squeezing my eyes shut, I waited for Ms. Vesper to provide me with instructions on what to do next. After some time passed, I peered through slits, before opening my eyes and looking around. Nothing. I was standing in the same white room.

No. Upon closer inspection, I noticed that this white room was significantly bigger than the one I initially entered. When I turned around to face the center, the black chaise had disappeared. I twirled around for a second time, expecting to see Ms. Vesper. She was not there.

"Hello?" I called out.

Where was the entrance? All four walls were identical. I looked up to realize that I was inside a pure white cage, the smooth white walls indistinguishable from the floor and ceiling. It was disorienting.

"Hello?"

Without warning, something plummeted from above and crashed onto the floor. It was a man, a gorgeous man.

Suspended upside down, he dangled from the ceiling, the intricate knots of the ropes carefully wrapped around his body like a work of art. His skin was a smooth, sun-kissed bronze, muscles sculpted as if chiseled by a master artist. Every line, every curve of his body exuded strength and grace. With a broad chest that tapered down, his abs were like a symphony of ripples, moving with every breath he took.

I couldn't help but let my eyes trace the patterns of the ropes, each knot and twist accentuating his physique rather than hiding it. The ropes crisscrossed over his chest, snaked around his arms, and wound down his legs, creating a mesmerizing lattice that both restrained and highlighted his form. Despite the unconventional position, his legs remained strong and defined, and his feet seemed completely at ease.

Even inverted, his features were striking. High cheekbones, a strong jawline, and full lips that seemed to invite attention. His eyes were closed, long dark lashes resting gently against his cheeks. His hair, a tousled dark mane, hung down towards the floor, adding to the surreal and hypnotic image before me.

My breath caught in my chest. I took him in inch by beautiful inch. With an air of tranquility, the man appeared to be completely at ease. It was second nature to him. The way he hung there, serene and composed, made it seem like he was an ethereal being, dropped into this realm from another.

My gaze traveled back up his body, lingering on the taut muscles of his arms and shoulders, the subtle flexing of his biceps as he maintained his balance. It was impossible to look away, every detail demanding attention, every inch of his skin drawing me in further.

Wandering up his body, I locked eyes on his exposed cock. Even in this upside-down state, it was impressive, his length hanging heavily, framed by the lines of the ropes. It was raw masculinity and vulnerable beauty. His cock was smooth and inviting.

The sheer audacity of his nakedness, coupled with his serene confidence, made my pulse quicken. It was an intimate and erotic vision stirring a deep, primal response within me. I couldn't peel my eyes away.

"Hello, Andrew," the man said. The sudden break in silence startled me, and I stumbled backward, falling to a seated position on the floor.

"Uhh…," I stammered. "Hello. Sorry. Hello. I, uh…"

The naked man smiled. "You have no need for embarrassment here." His smile, albeit upside down, was assuring and warm.

"This is your fantasy, Andrew. You are always in control of what does or doesn't happen here. Nevertheless, it is important to acknowledge that your presence here signifies a willingness to surrender control. I will be your guide through all of this. You are safe. My name is Julian, and I am here for you," he said, his gaze never leaving mine.

"Nice to meet you," I said, looking around.

"It's just you and me here," Julian said, soothing my unease. "You are safe with me. Okay?"

I nodded.

"You are in control," Julian repeated. "For now. We'll take some of that control away after you and I are completely comfortable, but only when you ask me to, okay?"

I nodded again. "What do I do?"

"What do you want to do?" he asked.

I glanced over my shoulder, then back at Julian, still hanging from the ceiling. I noted his suspension point disappeared into the ceiling with no knots.

I shrugged.

"Why don't we start," he suggested with a mischievous grin, "by shedding those garments? How does that make you feel?" Julian asked.

Fidgeting with my T-shirt collar, I cast another quick glance around me.

"It's just you and I, Andrew," Julian assured me again.

I tugged at my shirt and pulled it off over my head. My body was a stark comparison to Julian's. His physique was a masterpiece, every muscle defined, his skin smooth and unmarred. Although my own chest felt inadequate, there was a certain sense of freedom in exposing myself to him.

I could see a faint outline of my ribs beneath my skin, a reminder of my lean frame. A rush of vulnerability and excitement, my heart pounding in my chest.

With a sigh of relief, I released the breath I had been holding and gingerly reached for the waistband of my jeans. Despite my fumbling fingers, I was able to successfully undo the button. With a deliberate motion, I eased my jeans down, relishing the sensation of the cool air caressing my skin. I stepped out of them, standing there in just my underwear, feeling exposed but strangely empowered.

Julian's intense gaze remained fixed on me, his eyes like magnets drawing me closer, captivated by his unwavering attention. His presence was magnetic, and I wanted to please him, to show him everything. With a final, deep breath, I hooked my thumbs into the waistband of my underwear and slid them down, stepping out of them. I stood completely nude.

I stirred under his gaze and imagined my body through Julian's eyes. The feeling was thrilling and intimidating, a mix of excitement and apprehension.

There I stood, bare before him, my skin tingling with the coolness of the room and the heat of his eyes. Every inch of me on display, and for the first time, I felt a strange sense of liberation in my nudity.

"Why don't you step back over here, beautiful," Julian said.

A primal, animalistic lust shot through my veins. I moved forward.

"Closer."

Another step, and my face met his groin.

"Do you see how hard you make me?" he asked.

"Yes," I said, my mouth watering for his bulge.

"Do you want to put that in your mouth?" Julian asked, clearly knowing the answer already. "Be a good boy and take me whole."

I leaned forward, mouth opened and ready, and used my tongue to guide him inside of me without the use of my hands.

THREE

J ulian was a burst of sweet and salty. I eagerly tasted every inch of his girth, relishing the sensation of every ridge and vein under my tongue. The sound of Julian's pleasure-filled moan fueled the fire of passion, pushing me deeper. Another thrust of my mouth before releasing his member. I spit on my hand, grabbed his cock, and stroked it slowly until it slipped easily between my fingers.

I eagerly took him back into my mouth, using the motion of my hand to heighten his pleasure. He let out a feral growl, which made me stroke him faster and harder. I squeezed harder to increase the pressure and felt him swell even more.

"Slow down, baby. We've got all the time in the world," Julian whispered. I couldn't help it. I wanted to taste him completely. My mouth worked eagerly, savoring every moment. Julian's hand, now free, tangled in my hair, guiding me gently.

I pulled back slightly. In that fleeting moment, our eyes met, and it felt like time stood still. Julian's expression softened, his gaze full of warmth and desire. He cupped my face, his thumb tracing my lips.

"Let's take this slow," he murmured, his voice tender and sweet. He pulled his swinging body close to mine, the heat between us palpable. I met his lips and tasted the lingering sweetness of our kiss, savoring every second.

The awkwardness of him being upside down was growing apparent. "I think we're ready for the next level of intimacy. Give me a moment to get out of these ropes."

I took a step back, my eyes scanning the ceiling for any possible means to help him escape from his binds. There was no visible way to lower him to the ground and attempt to untangle the web that bound him. To my astonishment, I discovered him standing upright and unbound, with the ropes dangling loosely behind him as if they were mere afterthoughts.

"How did you..." I trailed off.

"Magic," he smiled coyly.

Julian reached for a hug. Closing the distance between us, he held me tightly in his arms. I melted between his powerful arms, feeling safe and desired. Something I'd never felt so wholly before. Julian's touch was gentle as he guided me. But my mind was a whirlwind of insecurity. What did Julian see in me?

Did he notice the scars, the imperfections, the stretch-marks, and love handles?

"You're safe with me," Julian whispered, sensing my hesitation. "There's nothing here but acceptance."

I took a deep breath, feeling a flicker of hope. Julian's words soothed my fears. For the first time, I felt a glimmer of trust, a tentative step towards opening up. His eyes held a warmth that melted away the cold grip of my past. Maybe, just maybe, I could let someone in.

While we embraced each other, the walls of the room seemed to shimmer and shift. Out of nowhere, a door appeared, a seamless part of the white expanse just moments before. Julian gently released me, took my hand, and led me toward the door.

We stepped through the door. The next room was a dark, rich red and black aesthetic. Luxurious fabrics draped the walls, absorbing the light and creating an intimate, almost mystical ambiance. In the center of the room was a large, comfortable-looking bed, its dark sheets and plush pillows inviting.

Julian's presence beside me was reassuring as I took in the new surroundings. The contrast between the stark white room and this dark, sensuous space was disorienting yet exhilarating.

"This is more like it," Julian said, his voice a low, seductive rumble. With a confident and fluid motion, he released his grip on my hand and gracefully made his way towards the bed. I followed, nervous anticipation bubbling inside me.

Julian turned to face me, his eyes gleaming with

mischief. "Are you ready to continue our adventure?" he asked, voice charged with promise.

I nodded. The intimacy of the moment, the closeness we shared, and the thrill of the unknown all combined to create a heady mix of emotions.

Julian took my hand again, pulling me close. His lips, warm and insistent, locked with mine in a deep and passionate kiss. As our bodies pressed together, I could feel the tension and desire building between us. The world outside this dark, alluring room ceased to exist. There was only Julian and the promise of what lay ahead.

We moved towards the bed together, the soft fabric of the sheets brushing against my skin as we climbed into it. Julian's hands roamed over my body, his touch electrifying.

He paused, his eyes locking onto mine. "Let's take our time," he whispered, his breath hot against my ear. "We have all the time we want."

The promise in his words thrilled me. We lay there, wrapped in each other's arms. Anticipation was almost overwhelming. This was more than just physical. We connected. Deep and undeniable, forged in magic.

With my finger, I traced the outline of his face, gently tickling with every stroke. I ran my finger around his perfect lips until desire was exploding inside of me, demanding more. I grabbed a fistful of hair and pulled him into me. We kissed, our tongues battling each other for space. The intensity of his desire was evident by his swollen member, stabbing me in the stomach.

He pulled me closer, our lips pressed together. He pushed me flat on my back and climbed on top of me. I couldn't help but revel in the feeling of his weight pressing into me.

"Are you ready for the next exercise?" Julian asked, still on top of me.

His face radiated beauty, and I couldn't resist the urge to run my fingers through his hair, savoring the softness as I lovingly stroked his ear. I couldn't imagine how this could get any better, but I nodded, ready for whatever was next.

"No more kissing," he said and smirked.

Despite the sinking feeling in my stomach, I chose to trust him. "Okay?"

"We're going to take turns exploring each other's bodies with our hands. No kissing. No sucking. No penetration," Julian explained.

I grinned. "Who's first?"

Four

Julian laid down on his stomach next to me. I turned onto my side, giving my right hand better access to his body. Anticipation coursed through my trembling fingers as they ventured across his broad back, tracing the contours of the firm muscle beneath his velvety skin.

Julian's skin radiated warmth under my touch. Using my fingertips, I delicately drew loops on his shoulders and followed the curves of his spine, paying attention to every rise and fall. His muscles relaxed beneath me, and I moved lower, letting my hand glide over his firm buttocks. I squeezed gently, marveling at the perfect firmness.

Continuing my exploration, I felt the strength of his powerful thighs beneath my hand. His legs exuded tension and power, the muscles rippling from his calves down to his feet. My fingers gently kneaded into the arch and toes of each foot, and Julian responded with soft, contented murmurs.

As I moved back up his legs, I couldn't help but be drawn to the curves of his ass again. Leaning in, I placed a soft kiss on the peak of his right cheek, tasting the salt of his skin. Suddenly, Julian tensed and turned his head slightly.

"Hands only, Andrew," he said firmly.

A wave of embarrassment washed over me, causing me to instinctively pull back. I'd broken the rules, so it was understandable. With a sigh, I released my breath and explored further, relying solely on the sensation of touch from my fingers. Taking in every inch of his body, memorizing the feel of his skin and the strength beneath it. The intimacy of the moment grew.

With each stroke, I could sense the steady ebb and flow of Julian's breath, syncing with my own. His contented sigh filled the room, as his body melted into an even deeper state of relaxation. I marveled at him, feeling a mixture of desire and admiration.

My hands moved back to the mounds of his ass, spreading his cheeks apart while I stuck my finger down his hairless crack. When I reached his hole, I gently massaged the outside with the tip of my middle finger. Julian flinched and his cheeks clamped down around my finger.

"Hey. I thought I was allowed as long as it was my hands," I said, my voice filled with the disappointment of a child who was just denied their favorite toy.

"Oh, it's allowed," Julian laughed, "but I'm also

very sensitive, and that was a completely involuntary clench."

"I see," I smirked and spread his ass even more open, exposing his hole to me. His anus, tight and inviting, drew me in. It was a point of both vulnerability and desire, a hidden pleasure waiting to be discovered. My finger hovered just above, feeling the heat emanating from him and the anticipation between us.

The tip of my finger outlined his hole once more, and he squirmed and moaned beneath my touch. This made me swell.

I wanted more.

With his cheeks spread open, I leaned in and spit just above his rosebud. The bead slipped down into his hole. I inserted the tip of my finger slowly, pulling out to allow more moisture inside. With a gentle touch, I slid my finger inside him, stopping when I made it to the first knuckle. He was warm and smooth, like a silk pillow. He let out a deep moan that verged on a growl. I continued further to the next knuckle. His hole tightened around my finger.

The more I pressed, the more I could sense the intense heat and tautness of his body completely enveloping my finger. Julian's moans grew louder, more desperate, as I explored him with a slow, deliberate rhythm. His reactions fueled my desire, and I found myself lost in the moment, captivated by the intimacy of this connection.

Julian's back arched slightly, his muscles tensing

and relaxing in response to my touch. I could feel the raw need radiating from him, and it spurred me on, making me want to pleasure him. In every movement, I listened to his body to understand what he needed.

I added another finger, slowly stretching him, preparing him. In that moment, Julian's breath hitched, and a deep, resonant moan escaped him, electrifying the air between us. I leaned in, my lips brushing against the small of his back, and felt him shiver beneath me.

"Watch those lips, Andrew," he murmured, and I backed off. He arched his back, allowing my fingers deeper inside of him. "More, please."

I obliged, working my fingers deeper, feeling his body's response to my touch. The restrictions placed upon me were driving me insane. Desire surged through me, intensifying with every passing second.

Julian's hips moved in time with my fingers, his body seeking more pleasure. I could tell he was close, the tension in his muscles reaching a peak. I wanted to bring him to the edge, to watch him experience the cliffs of pleasure.

Just as I was about to send him over the edge, Julian's eyes locked onto mine, filled with a raw, primal hunger. "Stop." His voice was firm but gentle. "Not yet."

I withdrew my fingers slowly, feeling the loss of warmth around them. Julian rolled onto his back, panting. His chest heaved with deep breaths. He pulled me down beside him, wrapping me with his arms.

"That was amazing," he whispered, his lips brushing against my ear. "But there's so much more I want to do with you."

FIVE

"It's your turn," Julian whispered, his lips barely grazing against my ear. With a gentle touch, he laid me down on my back and carefully positioned my arms above my head. "Get comfortable, but don't move."

I complied, feeling a surge of anticipation. I laid there, exposed and waiting for his touch. Julian's eyes devoured my body, a hungry glint in his gaze that sent a chill through my stomach. His hands were warm as they began their journey, starting at my neck.

He traced a line down my throat, his touch feather-light and teasing. My pulse quickened. His fingers moved lower, over my collarbones, and then spread out to my shoulders. His touch left me aching for more.

Julian's fingers danced over my chest, weaving through the hair that covered it. He played with my hair, tugging lightly, before moving on. His fingers grazed my nipples. I gasped as he pinched one, sending a jolt of pleasure straight to my groin.

Julian smirked, clearly enjoying the effect it had on me. "Stay still," he reminded me softly, his breath hot against my skin.

His hands trailed down, grazing my ribs before settling on my stomach. Julian took his time exploring the trail of hair that led from my navel south. He traced the line with his fingers, skirting around my cock, which strained with need.

My breath hitched as his hands traveled over my hips and down my thighs. He massaged the muscles there, his fingers digging in just enough for a groan to escape me. Julian's hands gently glided from my knees to my calves, their touch evoking a tender sensation that quickened my heartbeat.

Despite his demand to stay still, I found it increasingly challenging to resist the urge to move. His hands were everywhere, teasing and tantalizing, but never touching where I needed it most. My body was on fire, every nerve ending screaming for his touch.

Julian's hands moved to my feet, outlining every toe. He dragged his tip across my arches. I squealed and pulled back involuntarily at this. The sensation was maddening.

"Don't. Move," Julian playfully barked.

I released my knees and laid my legs back flat against the bed. Desire pooled in my stomach, a burning need that grew with each passing second. Julian worked his hands back up my legs and drew into my inner thigh. I wanted to squirm, but held strong—just as I was told.

"Julian," I whispered, my voice shaky. "Please…"

A wicked grin played at his lips. "Patience, Andrew," he tsked. "We're just getting started."

With deliberate slowness, he caressed my thighs, my calves, my ankles. Each touch sent sparks of pleasure through me. When he reached my hips, he traced around my cock, raking his fingers through my bush, gently scratching at the skin.

Finally, he brought his hands to my face, cradling it gently. He leaned down and held his lips above mine, his breath and the warmth of him hovering above me. I wanted to arch my neck off the pillow to meet his lips with mine, but somehow, I resisted the temptation. He outlined my lips with the tip of his finger, never pulling his face away from mine. Desire burned in his eyes, their depths filled with darkness and longing.

"I want you to remember every touch," he whispered. "Every moment."

I nodded, my heart pounding in my chest. Julian smiled and then began his teasing all over again, his hands exploring my body with a skill and tenderness that left me breathless.

"Flip over onto your stomach," Julian demanded.

I did as I was told. I adjusted my stiff cock to rest between my stomach and the warm mattress underneath.

Julian started at my shoulders, applying firm pressure to my muscles. His touch eased away any tension. He worked his way down my back, melting away any stress.

Julian's hands moved skillfully over my buttocks, applying a firm yet sensual pressure. His fingers kneaded the muscles, coaxing them to relax under his skilled touch. He placed soft kisses along the path.

"Hey, I thought it was hands only?" I pouted.

"Are you upset?" he teased.

"Absolutely not," I said, matching his energy.

"Good. Now be quiet and don't interrupt me, boy."

His forceful command did strange things to me. His words were uncomfortable, but somehow liberating. I can't describe why or what, but I knew one thing. I wanted more.

"Flip over," Julian commanded, and I complied, shifting on my back. He moved gracefully, his hands gliding over my body with a practiced ease.

He took my nipple in his mouth. My body quivered with delight as he gently sucked on my nipple, sending waves of pleasure pulsating through me. His teeth grazed my nipple with a gentle bite.

I let out an impulsive scream.

He stopped. "Are you okay?"

Gasping for air, I fought to find my voice and respond. I nodded. "Oh, yeah."

Julian smirked and moved to the other nipple. The sting of the bite sent a jolt of pain through my body, and I narrowly stifled another scream. I had never felt such a pleasurable pain.

As Julian completed the massage portion, he sat

back on his knees, his gaze meeting mine with a soft, reassuring smile. His hands rested lightly on my skin, a silent gesture of comfort and care. "How are you feeling?" he asked gently, his voice warm with concern.

"Amazing," I said with a sigh.

"I think you're ready for the next step," Julian said.

"Absolutely," I exclaimed, having no idea what was in store, but with Julian, I didn't care.

Julian's eyes sparkled with mischief. "The next step," he murmured, "is trust. Complete trust."

I swallowed hard, nodding. "I trust you."

He smiled warmly. "Good. Then close your eyes and let go."

Six

J ulian's command was clear and assertive, sending a thrill through me. "Spread your legs," he said.

I obeyed without hesitation, spreading my legs wider, offering myself completely to him.

"Good boy."

His words sent an explosion inside of my stomach, and I bit my lip to stifle a moan.

"You like that, don't you?" Julian asked, his voice soft yet commanding.

"Uh huh," I nodded, feeling a mixture of vulnerability and desire.

"When I call you a good boy?"

"Uh huh."

Julian wiggled his fingers as he moved slowly up my inner thighs, setting me ablaze. I moaned softly, the anticipation building with each touch. Julian paused and delicately tugged at my balls, sending pleasurable sensations radiating through my groin. He grabbed both with a single hand and stroked them in his palm, using his free fingers to tickle at the area just under my sack.

This made me squirm and open my legs wider to offer myself completely to him. He ran his hand back up my sack to the base of my shaft, tickling at the hair as he passed. He grabbed at my girth and slowly stroked, pulling my skin along.

I whimpered with pleasure, my hips pulsing in time with his strokes. Gently, with two fingers, he pulled my foreskin up over the tip and rolled it back down again. He repeated this action tirelessly, exerting a precise pressure that pushed me to the brink.

Before I could get there, he let go and my dick made a loud 'thwap' as it landed back on my stomach. Julian licked at my sack, sending tingles up my spine. He greedily sucked one inside his warm, wet mouth. He rolled it around, applying pressure between his tongue and the roof of his mouth.

Gently, he released it and did the same with my left nut. I squirmed on the inside, but was careful not to move away from him. I didn't want him to stop.

"That feels amazing," I assured him.

"You don't need to tell me. Your body is showing me," Julian explained. "Don't talk unless I tell you to."

I almost spoke to say, "Yes sir," but nodded instead.

"Good boy," he said and winked at me.

I threw my head back in pleasure at his words. He skillfully deepthroated my entire cock, leaving me gasping for breath. I nearly threw my back out, arching into him. As he took me all the way in, I could feel the tip brushing against the back of Julian's throat. His throat squeezed around me and I pulled out a little to provide him with relief.

To my surprise, he pulled me back in. The tightness pulsating on the edge of my cock was nearly too much. He backed out and then back in again, sending my middle into a frenzy.

A few more strokes and an explosion was forming deep within my sack. He slowly retreated, denying me the chance to find release.

I let out an exasperated sigh.

"It's not time yet, Andrew," Julian said. "We haven't begun the next level yet."

This surprised me. How much further could we go? I was about to give him my hot load directly into his throat.

"Sit up for me and lean back on the head of the bed," Julian commanded.

I did as I was told. Julian handed me a pillow to place in the small of my back. After I was comfortable, Julian spread my legs just wide enough so that he could sit in between them on his knees, his entire beautiful body exposed to me.

"I want you to take care of yourself," Julian said.

"How so?"

"I want to know what makes you tick," Julian explained. "We're going to be more verbal now. I'm going to tell you what I want you to do to yourself, and you're going to tell me what to do."

I smiled. "Okay. Grab your cock," I demanded.

"As you wish," Julian said. He grabbed his cock with his right hand. His girth filled his palm, and I raised my hand out to join him. He slapped it away.

"Nope, you want me to do something? You need to tell me, and I'll do it myself," Julian said.

"Okay, grab my hand and place it on your dick," I smiled with a cheeky grin.

"Haha, you're missing the point," Julian said.

"No, I'm not. I was trying to be funny," I smiled. "Stroke it for me."

Julian adhered to my command and started stroking himself. Long strokes that started at the base of his shaft and slowly moved out to the head, adding a little twist to the end, where the head meets the shaft. His twisted stroke left his cock, leaving his hand entirely. Julian used the head to break open the pressure that had formed by his closed fist. The stroke unfurled as it went slowly back down the shaft.

I licked my lips as I watched him. His eyes were locked onto me, stroking.

"Rub your other hand on your chest while you continue stroking," I ordered.

"Yes, Sir," Julian heeded. A hand met his navel and moved between his pecs. He gently caressed his right pec, his hand following the curves of his muscles around and around. His fingers gently brushed over his nipples in a circular motion.

His member stiffened with each stroke. His index finger and thumb worked gently at his left nipple, and he arched his back and sat up taller on his knees and locked eyes with me. He bit his lip, softly moistening his lips as he moaned.

"You like that?" he asked. The long strokes from his right hand continued.

"You are beautiful," I said, enjoying my show.

Julian smiled and then turned it on me. "Now, it's your turn. Show me how you like it."

I grabbed at myself and started stroking. To my delight, Julian never stopped stroking himself. I started stroking my tip almost exclusively, only every few strokes going the length of my shaft. Julian studied my cock and hand motions.

With my free hand, I began to tease and finger at my hole, intensifying the pleasure with each stroke. I adjusted my position so that my ass was more exposed for easier access. After moistening my fingers with spit, I carefully returned it to my hole. I ran my fingers along the circumference before sliding one inside. I remembered that this was the same finger that was inside of Julian, and it made me even more excited.

I moaned loudly.

"You like that, don't you?" Julian asked.

I nodded, barely able to speak with all of my senses alight.

"You're such a good boy, aren't you?" he asked.

"Oh fuck yes," I said, nodding slowly. This man learned all of my triggers just to exploit them.

"Are you ready for the next level, then?"

"Fuck yes," I begged.

SEVEN

J ulian pulled out a large box from the bedside table. It matched the theme of the room, mostly black with red metallic accents. He lifted the lid carefully and asked, "Do you trust me?"

"I do," I replied.

Julian pulled out ropes and laid them in front of me. My heart raced with nerves. Julian must have sensed my distress because he stopped unpacking the ropes.

"We don't have to do anything you're not comfortable with," he reassured.

"I know. I want to," I said.

"I'm glad to hear it," he smiled, and I melted. Any fear I had melted with it. Once again, my heart raced, but this time it was with excitement.

Julian took the first set of ropes and gently guided my arms above my head. He secured one wrist, his fingers working deftly as he tied the knots firmly. He moved to the other wrist, his touch careful and considerate.

"How does that feel?" he asked, his voice soothing.

"Good," I said, testing the bonds. They were secure but not painful, allowing a slight range of motion.

Julian moved to my feet, wrapping the ropes around each ankle and securing them to the corners of the bed. As he worked, he maintained eye contact, ensuring I was comfortable every step of the way.

"Remember, if at any point you want to stop, just say the word," he said.

"I will," I promised, appreciating the concern.

With my limbs bound, Julian leaned back, admiring his work. He then climbed onto the bed beside me, his hands gently tracing the ropes on my skin.

He worked his way down to my stomach, hands moving in slow, purposeful circles. I closed my eyes, losing myself to the sensation. He moved to my arms, massaging from my shoulders down to my wrists, carefully around the ropes. He took his time, ensuring every inch of my skin was attended to.

A surge of warmth and comfort moved through me, knowing I was in safe hands. Julian's presence was reassuring, his touch exhilarating. He leaned in closer, gently kissing my neck.

"You're doing great," he whispered. "Just relax and enjoy."

I let out a contented sigh, surrendering to the

moment. The world outside ceased to exist, and all that mattered was Julian and his touch.

Julian continued to move his hands skillfully over my body, his touch tender and firm. He ran his fingers through my chest hair, tugging gently. He moved back up to my shoulders, working out my knots with practiced ease, sending waves of relaxation and desire through me.

His hands traveled down my sides, each touch barely a graze against the sensitive skin there. I squirmed. The sensation was extremely ticklish. I caught myself sucking in and holding my breath.

Julian's smooth voice calmed me. "Just breathe, Andrew," he whispered, lips close to my ear. "Let go."

I obeyed, focusing on my breath, letting the air in my chest melt away. Julian's hands moved lower, massaging my thighs with a firm but gentle grip. He worked each muscle with care, his touch knowing and skilled.

He let up the pressure and started tickling at my feet. Unable to recoil from his attacks, I arched my back as far as I could, laughing and squirming. Julian kept at it and smiled with delight.

Julian paused at my middle, leaning in to kiss the shaft of my cock, then moved down and kissed each of my balls. He then rubbed his five o'clock shadow against the sensitive skin of my hard-on. Each kiss and movement was soft, almost reverent. A pulsating rush of pleasure ran up and down my spine.

He opened his mouth, licked my tip, and took me

all the way inside his mouth. He thrust gently and swiftly, focusing concertedly on the tip. I squirmed once again, which made him take me in deeper.

Julian gently let me go and ran his tongue down the length of my shaft to my sack. He ran his tongue back and forth between my two stones until they were wet with his moisture. Contained by the ropes, I arched my body, feeling the tension in every muscle.

His rough stubble grazed my skin, causing me to let out an unexpected squeal of delight.

"Mmmm, someone liked that, huh?" Julian asked.

"Yes, sir." I arched off the bed, exposing my ass to him.

Julian let out a menacing growl and sank his body lower onto the bed. He arched his body into an inner thigh stretch between my legs, his shoulders pinning my thighs as wide as they could go with my ankles restrained. He wrapped his arms underneath me so that my ass was lifted off the bed and completely exposed to him.

Julian's hands rested on the top of my legs. He tickled close to my sack with his tongue. I squirmed. There was no way for me to move, except for scooting my ass closer to his face. His lips gently brushed against the sensitive skin of my lower inner thigh.

"Eat that ass," I said.

"Beg me." Julian kissed at my inner thigh again, this time on my left side.

"Please."

"What?"

"Please sir, eat that ass," I begged.

"You want me to eat this ass?" He kissed my exposed hole.

"Oh fuck yes, please."

Julian moved in closely, positioning his face near my ass as his tongue expertly explored every inch, paying particular attention to my crack. I let out a loud moan and felt my dick swell. I could feel his tongue gently exploring my entrance. His stubble rubbing against my split. Determined, I attempted to lower myself even more onto his face, seeking a better position.

His tongue punched at my hole, and I relaxed to let it inside. He moved it rhythmically while inside of me, and a flash of ecstasy filled my center.

I screamed out. "I need you now. Please, take me!"

A mischievous grin stretched across Julian's face. "Now we're talking."

EIGHT

J ulian sat up in the bed and adjusted himself to
his knees. He grabbed at his engorged shaft and
slapped it against mine.

"Is this what you want?" he teased.

"Yes, please," I cried.

"You want this inside of you?" he jiggled his
thick, veiny rod up and down and slapped it against
my thigh.

"Please, I need you. I can't take it anymore,
please. Please, sir," I begged.

Leaning over me, his face loomed inches away
from mine. "You're a good boy, and I love how good
you beg for this cock," he said, and he kissed me. I
took him in, feeling his body against mine.

"Fuck me, please," I truly begged this time. The
suspense was too much to bear.

Julian let his heat-seeking missile find my hole.
Then, gently, he forced his way inside. My head shot

backward as the initial shock set in. He held position while my body adjusted to his bulging cock.

"You doing okay?" he asked, looking for reassurance.

"Fuck yes." I shifted to take him in deeper.

"You are quite the eager one, aren't you?" he smiled his saucy grin.

I nodded.

He slid in further.

I gasped as I took him all the way inside of me. Julian held once more. Once my stomach had relaxed again, he thrusted. With slow, deliberate movements, he moved inside me. In and out. My eyes rolled back into my head, overwhelmed by the intensity.

He thrusted inside of me, his sack clapping against me. I screamed out in pleasure as I took him in, repeatedly. I wished I could reach down and stroke my cock as he pumped deeper and deeper inside of me.

Then, as if he was reading my thoughts, he reached down and grabbed ahold of my girth, stroking me with careful consideration of the head. My breathing quickened. I felt an explosion building from inside of me. I held my breath. He thrust harder and stroked me faster.

He licked his other hand, spit filling his palm. Switching hands, he continued stroking me. Julian's breath became more labored, matching my own.

Faster.

And faster.

My breath was stolen from me. The explosion

inside of me was too much to hold on to. I let out a primal howl as my release erupted, splattering across my chest and stomach. Julian continued stroking. My body convulsed uncontrollably. The cascading fluid dripped down his knuckles while he thrusted inside me.

Two more thrusts and his head flew back in exultation, his heat exploding inside of me. Julian's body quivered with excitement, and he let out a primal growl of pleasure. When he could breathe normally again, he looked down at his knuckles covered in my juices. He delicately licked his finger, removing every trace of my cum.

He pulled himself from me and collapsed on top of me. Our combined moisture flowed together in a cold soup between our hot skin. We both writhed and shook as the aftershocks of pleasure rocked through our bodies. He kissed me, and I tasted myself on his tongue, sweet and tangy.

Julian flopped down beside me, running his hands over my nipples and through my chest hair. His right leg draped over my body, wrapping me in an embrace.

"I'm so proud of you. You were amazing," he whispered in my ear.

I wanted to hold him, but my hands and feet were still bound. I was completely helpless and vulnerable to him.

Julian noticed my struggle and chuckled softly. "Let me take care of that," he said, reaching for the knots that held me captive. His fingers worked expertly, and soon the ropes fell away, freeing me from my restraints.

I flexed my wrists and ankles, feeling the circulation return. Julian's hands moved gently, massaging the areas where the ropes had been, soothing the slight soreness.

"Thank you," I purred, wrapping my arms around him now that I could. The sensation of his warm body against mine was comforting.

Intimate.

He kissed my forehead tenderly, his lips lingering for a moment before he found my eyes. "You're welcome," he purred with a soft smile. "It was an incredible experience."

We lay there for a while, enjoying the closeness and the shared warmth. The night was quiet, the room dimly lit by the soft glow of the bedside lamp. Julian and I lay there, our bodies intertwined. The intensity of the evening had given way to a peaceful stillness, a perfect moment to reflect on everything that had happened.

"You know," Julian began, his voice gentle, "the voices from our past only have the power we give them."

I turned to face him, his words striking a chord deep within me. "What do you mean?"

Julian squeezed my hand, his eyes searching mine. "Those moments of hurt and rejection, they don't define you unless you let them. You've been carrying memories like weights, but you don't have to. You can choose to let them go."

I felt a lump form in my throat as his words sank in. "It's hard," I admitted. "Those voices, they've been with me for so long."

Julian nodded, understanding in his eyes. "I know it's not easy. But look at how far you've come. You've faced your fears, opened up, and let someone in. That's growth, Andrew. You're stronger than you think."

I thought back to all the moments of vulnerability, the times I wanted to run but stayed. The echoes of high school rejection, the humiliation from college, Adonis in the alleyway, they felt distant now, like shadows losing their grip.

"You're right," I said softly. "I've been letting those voices control me for too long."

Julian smiled, a warmth that reached his eyes. "You have the power to rewrite those narratives. To see yourself not through their eyes, but through your own. Through mine."

I took a deep breath, feeling a weight lift off my shoulders. "Thank you, Julian. For everything."

He leaned in, pressing a gentle kiss to my forehead. "You did this, Andrew. You found the strength within yourself. I'm just here to remind you of what you're capable of."

As we lay there, the past no longer felt like a chain holding me down. Instead, it was a part of my story, one that I could learn from and move beyond. I knew the journey wasn't over, but for the first time, I felt a sense of peace. A belief in my own strength and worth.

"I'm ready," I whispered, more to myself than to Julian. "I'm ready to let go."

Julian's smile widened, his eyes shining with pride. In that moment, I knew I was no longer defined by the voices of my past. I was defined by the choices I made, the love I embraced, and the strength I found within myself. And with Julian by my side, the future felt brighter than ever.

Eventually, Julian sighed and sat up. "I suppose it's time to say goodbye," he said, a hint of reluctance in his voice.

I nodded, feeling a pang of sadness but also a sense of fulfillment. "Until next time," I replied.

Julian leaned in for one last kiss, slow and lingering, savoring the moment. "Until next time," he echoed, his eyes filled with promise.

With a final smile, he stood up and started dressing. I followed suit, the weight of the experience sinking into my bones and etching itself into a treasured memory.

"Take care, Andrew," he breathed.

"You too, Julian." I walked out of the room feeling a mixture of exhilaration, contentment, and sorrow. Already looking forward to the next encounter, I wondered if I truly would ever see him again. The white room got brighter and brighter until the brightness blinded me completely.

NINE

I gently opened my eyes and found myself in the small white room, laying on the black chaise. My return to The Arcane Room was disorienting and peaceful all at the same time. A small rush of embarrassment flooded through me when I remembered I had Larissa to contend with in the next room. She would ask me every detail of my encounter.

The memory of Julian's words resurfaced, emphasizing the exclusivity of our experience—it was something shared only between us. I relaxed.

"So, how was it?" Ms. Vesper asked with a sly smile.

I hadn't realized she was there. "Incredible." I couldn't contain the ear-to-ear smile. As we exited the white room and walked back into the main part of the store, I saw Larissa.

Before she interjected, I asked, "How much do I owe you?"

Ms. Vesper chuckled, a mischievous glint in her eyes. "The first time is free, but gratuities are always welcome."

I nodded, feeling grateful. I reached into my wallet and handed her a generous tip. "Thank you, Ms. Vesper. It was truly an unforgettable experience."

Larissa was waiting for me, her eyes wide with curiosity. "Wow, you look... different," she remarked, tilting her head. "What happened in there?"

I gave her a knowing smile. "It's your turn to find out," I said, gesturing towards the table with the tarot deck.

Her eyes lit up with excitement and a bit of apprehension. "Really? You think I should?"

"Absolutely," I encouraged her. "It's an experience you don't want to miss."

Ms. Vesper stepped forward, placing a comforting hand on Larissa's shoulder. "Ready to explore, my dear?"

Larissa glanced at me one last time before nodding eagerly. "Okay, let's do this."

As Ms. Vesper guided Larissa toward the table, I watched them go, feeling a sense of satisfaction. The Arcane Room had already changed my life, and I knew it was about to do the same for Larissa.

Julian's words and the journey we'd shared had given me a fresh perspective. I knew that this was just the beginning of a new chapter in my life, one where I embraced my true self and let go of the past.

The Arcane Room had opened a door within me,

and I was eager to walk through it, knowing that I was no longer bound by the shadows of my past.

Sign up for Jax Wilder's newsletter and receive a collection of unpublished Coral Cove short stories. Meet familiar characters and dive deeper into the love and romance that Coral Cove is known for. Don't miss out on this exclusive content!

Jax Wilder

You can also join Rainbow Quartz Publishing's Newsletter:

**Rainbow Quartz
Publishing**

If you enjoyed *Hanged Passions,* I hope you check out *Harvesting Love* from the Coral Cove series.

Ben
It's the anniversary of my fiancé's death and a weekend in Coral Cove was to honor the trip we never got to take. So, is it wrong that I'm falling into bed with the cute bookstore clerk? The chemistry is undeniable. But am I ready to embrace the magic has to offer?

Park
Being best friends with the boss has its perks, like a discount on the latest spicy MM romance and the ability to knock off a bit early when a smokin' hot bibliophile pops into the shop. Thanksgiving is more about family anxiety than holiday cheer, until a chance encounter with good taste changes every-

thing. Can I convince him to spend a little more time together, even if it's with my crazy family?

Step into Coral Cove, where the magic of Thanksgiving brings love and passion to life in this heartwarming and tantalizing MM romance.

A man scarred by loss, looking for a fresh start in Coral Cove. His chance meeting with Park in the quaint bookstore sparks more than just friendly conversation.

When Park and Ben's paths cross, the chemistry is instant and undeniable. What begins as an innocent meeting soon turns into a night of passion.

ALSO BY JAX WILDER

Lorelai Hamilton

Find Your Bliss

Teenage Witch's Grimoire

Tarot Reflection Journal

Tarot Refection Journal Coloring The Tarot

The Eclectic Witch's Grimoire

Dream Journal

Teenage Tarot

Tarot Tales and Magic Spells

Arcane In Verse

Isla Watts

A Fairy Bad Day

Surprise! You're a Vampire

Gorgeous, Gorgeous, Gorgons

Mork The Handsome Orc

Adopted By Werewolves

Bite Me If You Can

That's The Spirit!

Rose Dawson's Book Journals

My Time With The Fairies

Enchanted Escapades

Enchanted Escapades

Dewey Decimal Diaries

Siren's Songbook

Pride and Prejudice

Bibliophile's Bounty

Book of Books Journal

Pages & Passages Reading Journal

Bookworm's Companion Reading Journal & Tracker

ABOUT THE AUTHOR

Jax Wilder is a passionate romance author hailing from a charming small town nestled in the picturesque Pacific Northwest. With a heart full of love and an unyielding belief in the power of happily ever afters, Jax weaves enchanting tales of love and connection that leave readers captivated.

Jax's novels are a reflection of her commitment to celebrating the magic of love, and her characters' journeys mirror the warmth and happiness she has found in her own life. Join her on the enchanting journey of love, passion, and enduring connection through her heartfelt romance novels.

Made in the USA
Columbia, SC
12 November 2024

45955683R00039